Storylandia

The Wapshott Journal of Fiction

Issue 32

The Wapshott Press

Storylandia, Issue 32, The Wapshott Journal of Fiction, ISSN 1947-5349, ISBN 978-1-942007-28-9 is published at intervals by the Wapshott Press, now a 501(c)(3) nonprofit, PO Box 31513, Los Angeles, California, 90031-0513, telephone 323-201-7147. All correspondence can be sent to The Wapshott Press, PO Box 31513, LA CA 90031-0513. Visit our website at www.WapshottPress.org to learn more. This work is copyright © 2020 by Storylandia. The Wapshott Journal of Fiction, Los Angeles, California. Copyright © 2019 J.H. Malone and is reprinted here with the copyright owner's permission.

Storylandia is always seeking quality original short stories, novelettes, and novellas. Please have a look at our submission guidelines at www.Storylandia.WapshottPress.org or email the editor at editor@wapshottpress.org

Donations happily accepted at donate.wapshottpress.org

Cover image by Eadweard Muybridge, www.bit.ly/2OJuZ2X

Storylandia

The Wapshott Journal of Fiction

Founded in 2009

Issue 32, Winter 2020

Edited by Ginger Mayerson

Drunk on Time

By J.H. Malone

Drunk on Time

by
J.H. Malone

Drunk on Time

Mildred McGarvey ate a muffin while working on her memoirs in the activity room. Crumbs fell from her lips and gummed up her keyboard. The t and h keys. She brought the laptop out to me in the center's office with an embarrassed look on her face. I turned it upside down and shook it. Crumbs fell out. Others stayed put. I picked up my can of compressed air.

Just then Valeria Garza appeared at the center's double doors. She banged on one of them and Fred Barnes hustled over to pull it open for her. She pushed past him with a grunt, spotted me in the office, and hobbled toward me on her bad hip.

I dislodged a crumb with a blast from the can. Valeria tapped me on the shoulder.

"Saul," she said.

"No tapping," I said.

"I've gotta talk to you."

"Soon as I'm done with this laptop," I said.

"He's helping me," Mildred said.

"Wait outside," Valeria said to her. "This is personal."

Mildred stepped out and Valeria pushed the door shut.

"Get done please," she said.

I held up my hand. She took my sleeve between thumb and bony forefinger and gave it a tug.

"You're the big computer expert," she said. "I

need your help and I need it fast."

I blew crumbs.

"I'm gonna tell you something," Valeria said, "which is strictly between you, me, and the bedpost. Understand?"

"My lips are sealed," I said.

"My granddaughter Julieta, she's seventeen. She's seeing a guy who's trouble."

I put down my can.

"His name is Tommy Link," Valeria said. "Julieta thinks she's in love. Tommy is nineteen, maybe twenty."

"Okay."

"Her dad told her to stop seeing the boy, but she just left the house with him. She had an overnight bag. They got in his car and took off."

"That doesn't sound good."

"Running off with Tommy is the worst thing she could do. My son has a temper."

"Have you tried calling her?"

"She don't answer."

"So why tell me?"

"I want you to find out where she's gone and what she's doing."

She pointed at the laptop.

"Valeria," I said, "this is Mildred's computer. She's waiting for it. And how am I supposed to find out what your granddaughter is doing on a laptop? I don't know her and I don't know the boy. I've got nothing to go on. I can find you a good surgeon for that hip, but your granddaughter's social life is something else entirely."

"Use Facebook," Valeria said. "Use Twitter. Use those other things the kids use. SpotAndFly. Google her. Google Tommy's license plates. Email her. Text her. Do like they do on TV and hack her. Hack them both. What are you asking me for? You're the expert. Everybody says you can find anything on the computer. You've got a gift. Track her down. Go on now."

She pulled out a picture of a teenager and waved it in front of me. A pretty young woman.

I opened my mouth but nothing came out. I wanted to say no, but the woman was desperate.

"You helped Malika Tory find her cat," she said. "You told Agnes Chang whose dog was pooping on her lawn."

I kicked myself for those mensch-like actions. No good deed.

"I know you're a slacker," Valeria said, "but show some gumption for a change. Quit lollygagging and get busy."

"I just fixed this laptop," I said. "What about that?"

"I'm sorry. Your lack of ambition is none of my business."

"I'll look into it," I said, "but I can't do anything on this machine. My search tools are on my computer at home. Mildred wouldn't want me snooping around your granddaughter on her laptop anyway."

I stood up.

"What can you tell me about Tommy?" I said.

She grabbed my hands. Hers were cold, despite the warmth of the day.

"He's a nice kid. He met Julieta when he was doing some business with Tony my son. They hit it off. Tommy is okay but he's having some serious business problems with Tony. I don't know where Tommy lives. I think he works at the IKEA in Burbank. He used to."

"What kind of serious business problems?"

Valeria rubbed thumb and forefinger together.

"Something's going on you're not telling me about," I said.

She stood looking at me, listing to the left.

"I'll see what I can find out," I said. "I'll be here for a while tomorrow before I go over to Hesby Seniors in Sherman Village."

"Call me as soon as you know something. I've got to talk to Julieta before she does something stupid and her dad finds out."

After showing Valeria out of the office, I gave Mildred her restored laptop and sat down to look up the Garza address. At five o'clock, I rolled out of the center's parking lot in my Jeep. I considered driving straight home and finding the missing couple but instead I headed over to The Studio, a dive on Magnolia in North Hollywood. I parked on the curb and swung my door open when the traffic was clear.

The Studio was my bar of choice when I wasn't in the mood to drink alone. It was located a couple of blocks from my apartment, which made it convenient when I was too impaired to drive home at the end of an evening.

The smell of stale beer greeted me at the door. I stood inside for a moment, letting my eyes adjust to the gloom, and then walked over and sat down at the end of the bar. Walt brought over a bowl of pretzels and a draft. Several of the regulars lifted their glasses and I toasted them back. I was the only one in the bar under sixty. Like at work.

"How're the old folks?" Walt said.

"Most of them younger than you are," I said.

I drank off half the beer. In back, Abe and Jose, both over eighty and arthritic, were playing a game of foosball that progressed at the speed of a zen exercise.

Mimi came in through the back and put on an

apron. Walt waved us a goodbye, gave his daughter a hug, and went out the way Mimi had come in.

She rubbed down the bar with a rag.

"You want a sandwich?" she said to me.

"Just an egg."

She brought over a bowl of hard-boiled eggs. I took one.

"How was your day?" she said.

"Valeria Garza wants me to find out what her granddaughter is up to. You know Julieta Garza?"

"I know her sister Mariana. We were in high school together. Julieta was just a kid at the time. What's Valeria worried about?"

"I think Julieta is hanging out with a kid who owes her dad money."

"Why does Valeria think you would know anything about Julieta?"

"I've used the internet a couple of times to help her friends at the center. Apparently I have a reputation."

"I'm older than Valeria Garza," Keishi Suzuki said, down the bar. "Why don't you ever help me?"

"What do you need?" I said.

"Another drink, but I'm tapped out."

I nodded to Mimi. She set Suzuki up with a shot.

"Nurse it," she said to him.

"We're drinking my rent money," I said to Suzuki.

"That's why it tastes so god-damned good," he said. "Always better when you don't pay for it."

"You know he's not broke," Mimi said to me.

I peeled and ate my egg and washed it down with the rest of the beer. Took a second egg from the bowl and got off my stool.

"Good luck with Julieta," Mimi said.

"Give me one more shot and put it on his tab," Suzuki said to her.

Outside, May twilight softened the urban scene with purple. Down the block, a homeless guy named Jekell sat with his back against the brick front of a laundry, his dog Bush beside him. Bush wagged his tail. I walked over and gave him the egg, which he wolfed down shell and all.

Magnolia Boulevard was still busy with folks heading home from work. I waited for a guy on a bike to whizz past, then climbed into the Jeep and fired it up.

I turned off Magnolia at Vineland. My apartment was a fifth-floor walkup in a vintage structure built long before the Metro Orange Line began gentrifying the area.

Inside, I broke open a fresh bottle of cheap bourbon and sat down at my work table in the apartment's second bedroom. I began my late-night granddaughter search by hitting the switch that powered up the scanner's server in its rack against the wall. Its auxiliary unit woke up next to it. I filled a water glass with bourbon and took a sip. Turned on the console and typed in the Garza address I had looked up in the Lankershim office. Took a sip. Settled the controller on my lap. One more sip and I pulled on my VR headset and snugged up its straps. My mouth was left free for my drink.

Inside the headset, a virtual 3D view phased in. I saw myself from behind. I twitched the joystick and the view drifted up to the ceiling, backing away toward the door.

I kept a list of bookmarks on the scanner. Before tracking the Garza girl, I took a minute to hop back for the thousandth time to the day I first laid eyes on Liesl.

Dr. Liesl Blau, recently arrived from Germany. On loan to MIT for a semester from the Max Planck Institute for Gravitational Physics in Potsdam-Golm. Looking like a teenager, she had already published a series of original papers in quantum cosmology and quantum gravity that rocked the scientific world and elevated the integration of gravitational and quantum physics into new realms. The University was abuzz at her arrival.

I was working on my fourth year as a support engineer in the University's IS&T department. We had set up Dr. Blau's office in Building 6, sandwiched between those of two Nobel physicists.

Dr. Liesl Blau, genius, live, on-campus.

"I am not a genius," she said to me once. "I have had one good idea."

"Einstein only had two," I said, "or so he told someone."

"Einstein changed the world. I will not."

She paused.

"I could," she said, "but I will not."

The scanner bookmark jumped me to the hallway outside her office, thirty seconds before I was due to show up. She opened her office door and stood waiting for me, a cup of coffee in her hand. No sound. She never got around to implementing sound on the scanner. She learned to read lips instead.

She looked younger than the students walking by. Younger, but like someone who knew things. Like a child standing in a bomb crater.

I took a sip and sat back in my chair. Behind her, outside her office window, the day was gray. She was wearing a German wool cardigan with the head of a stag or antelope or reindeer on its right side. I never asked her which. The passing students tried not to stare but failed. She watched the hall in the direction of Building 8. I paused the scan. Thirty seconds. All I allowed myself. I didn't need to see me. I needed to see her.

At this point I quit sipping and started drinking.

I had a granddaughter to snoop. I used the map feed and keyed in the Garza home coordinates on Pine Hill Drive in Shadow Hills. The scanner jumped to the location with its clock set back to noon, five hours before Valeria Garza showed up at the senior center. The house was a sprawling two-story job with stone siding and an artificial waterfall and rock swimming pool off to the right. Valeria's mother-in-law cottage was located on the opposite side of the house.

I scanned forward in time, increasing the scan speed while I watched for motion. A man zipped by, walking his dog. A classic Cutlass muscle car pulled in from the street onto the natural stone pavers in front of the house. I slowed the scan. A young man climbed out of the car. Tommy Link, I assumed. He hustled up to the front door and gave the silver knocker a good rap. He was a tall, blond, athletic-looking kid. The teenager in Valeria's photo opened the door. I didn't bother following Tommy in. I turned up the scan speed and freshened my drink instead. Presently Tommy came out with Julieta in tow. She was wearing a backpack and carrying a gym bag. The two of them were laughing.

Valeria Garza appeared at a window in her cottage as the couple walked to the car. This was minutes after four o'clock. Julieta glanced back and saw her grandmother and stopped laughing. Valeria tried to open the window but the Cutlass pulled out of the driveway while she struggled with it. No seatbelts in sight.

I manipulated the controller and followed the car around the big curve on McBroom to Sheldon, then to Roscoe and the Hollywood Freeway south to Chandler. The Cutlass made its way over to an LA Fitness on Coldwater Canyon, next to Tujunga Wash, two and a half miles from my apartment. After two hours of racquetball with a break in the middle, the couple showered, got back on the freeway and crawled south in rush-hour traffic to Little Armenia in East Hollywood. It took them more than an hour to get there. They were relaxed, in no hurry.

They had a leisurely dinner at a Lebanese restaurant on Hollywood Boulevard. No alcohol. Tommy kept an eye on his watch. When they were done and back in the car, they drove straight down Normandie to Wilshire in Koreatown. They parked in a church lot and Julieta waited in the car, smoking, while Tommy entered the church and joined a Gamblers Anonymous meeting in session.

I upped the scan rate. The meeting broke up and Tommy spent some time talking to a fellow who looked to be in his forties. Tommy's sponsor?

Night had fallen. With Tommy back in the car, the couple drove to a ritzy Los Feliz neighborhood above Little Armenia. Their destination was a stucco pile probably owned by a movie star back in the Thirties. The structure sat on a hillside behind a high wall on Glendower Avenue, near the slope that runs up to Griffith Observatory.

Tommy parked the Cutlass alongside several sports cars, models too expensive for me to recognize, outside a four-car garage. The couple went into the house hand-in-hand. Julieta's bag and backpack remained in the car. I didn't bother to follow them in. I was tired and drunk. I upped the framing rate and watched various other couples arrive. As the evening in my headset wore on, I waited for Tommy and Julieta to leave. The scanner reached the present moment, ten-thirty, with them still in the house. Early for them but I was ready for bed.

I backed up five minutes and scanned through the front door into the house. A long hall beyond a wide entryway led past stairs and a dining room, through double doors to a veranda in back. Slate steps descended to a deck and a pool in the shape of an hourglass. Couples were scattered around the pool drinking, smoking, snorting and getting physical.

Tommy and Julieta passed a joint back and forth, lying in a double lounge chair and talking to a couple doing the same next to them. I powered off the scanner, unstrapped my headset, and called Valeria.

"Who is this?" she said after ten rings. "I was asleep. It's the middle of the night."

"It's Saul and it's not even eleven yet. You told me to call you when I found Julieta."

"Have you been drinking?"

"Yes."

"Well, never mind. Have you found them? Where are they? What are they doing?"

"When they left your house this afternoon, they drove over to a gym and played racquetball. They had dinner at a restaurant. They went to a party in Los Feliz. They're there now."

"Facebook," Valeria said. "These kids report everything they do."

After accepting her profuse thanks, I drained my glass and made it to bed without incident.

At Lankershim in the morning, Valeria came in

and informed her friends that her daughter had not been misbehaving but did have boyfriend problems. Reaction to this news was mixed. Meanwhile, my reputation as an internet magician took another step up.

"They seemed good together," I said.

Valeria handed me a jar of plum preserves.

"From one of our trees," she said. "It's dropping fruit like crazy. I'm singing your praises this morning. I'm telling everyone."

I put the preserves aside and drank from my can of Sprite hangover medicine. I had several urgent requests for internet assistance as the Garza story got around.

I left for the Hesby Senior Center in Sherman Village at noon. I was servicing five facilities, being the principal IT tech for Cedros Senior Activity Centers, Inc., leader of senior enrichment in the Valley. By the time I went out to my Jeep in the lot, my headache was restricted to the floor of my brain and the Sprite wanted company in my stomach. I stopped at a McDonald's on my way over to Sherman Village and parked in the shade of an acacia tree. I bought a Big Mac and while I ate it in the Jeep, I thought about Tommy and Julieta. They impressed me as an intelligent, healthy couple of kids in love, which of course led my thoughts back to Liesl.

I was sent over to Liesl's office for the first time soon after her arrival, to help her with credentialing problems on her machine. As I came down the hall, I saw her standing in her office doorway with a cup of coffee in her hand. Her gaze had me by the eyes fifty feet away. She put out her free hand as I walked up.

"Dr. Blau," I said, taking it. "I'm your IT guy."

She had a grip.

"I know who you are," she said, sounding like Werner Herzog's granddaughter. "The problem is already solved."

Several gawking students slowed to listen. Dr. Blau let go of my hand and motioned them away with a quick gesture. She saw the look on my face.

"They are students," she said, as if that explained everything.

"Then I guess..."

She smiled and turned back into her office, closing the door behind her.

I stood there for a moment in case she opened it again. She didn't.

Magisterial. When I scanned her standing in the doorway waiting for me, I always stopped before the smile. I couldn't handle the smile.

At the end of that first day, I sat in my Jeep at an exit in the Stata Garage, waiting to pull out onto Vassar Avenue. Rain pelted down from a whale-gray sky. A woman in a bright blue raincoat crossed in front of me. She tilted her umbrella into the wind and I recognized Dr. Blau. Easing the Jeep out onto Vassar, I rolled up beside her as she strode along. I lowered the passenger-side window.

"Doctor, can I give you a ride?" I called.

She stopped and faced the car.

"I am too wet."

"It's an old car. Wet doesn't matter."

She climbed in, furling her umbrella. I put the Jeep in gear.

"In Pottsdam I walk home," Dr. Blau said.

"It's going to get colder," I said.

"MIT gives me a car and driver but I walk. In Pottsdam I walk home in the cold."

"Where is Pottsdam, exactly?"

"Close to Berlin."

She gave me an address on Washington Street. I took a left on Main and a right on Portland, and drove over to Washington. I kept my speed down with scientific royalty in the car.

"You are the IT fellow," she said.

"Saul," I said.

"Thank you for this ride. The wind pulls my umbrella."

"My pleasure," I said. "How are you liking MIT so far, and your time in America?"

"It is not so different from the Planck Institute. I knew already many of the faculty here."

"Everyone is excited to have you on campus."

"Yes."

Scientists, at MIT anyway, are not a modest lot.

I pulled up at the address she had given me, a restored triple-decker crowded between two wooden apartment buildings full of students. The tri-decker was one of those old homes in Cambridge built before World War I.

Rain drummed on the Jeep's roof. I turned to look at my passenger. She was staring at me. Her eyes seemed a little wide.

"What is it?" I said.

"You will come upstairs with me? I offer you a drink," she said.

"A drink?" I said. I am not a guy often asked up for a drink. This was Dr. Liesl Blau speaking to me, a new star in the cosmological firmament. A young star.

However, saying no was not an option. I wasn't qualified to carry her slide rule but science did not seem to be on her mind. I seemed to be on her mind.

Still, I hesitated. I knew how to have a good

time, but I wasn't sure I should try to have one with Einstein's daughter.

"My request is reasonable, yes?" she said. "I am a professor but also a woman. You are a man."

"Holy cow, Dr. Blau... How old are you?"

"Twenty-five."

"I'm twenty-five. You seem younger. And older."

"In Germany I live at home with my parents. I go too fast?"

She said this with a kind of familiar affection, the opposite of her nervous eyes, and put a hand on my arm.

"You're famous," I said, "an honored guest of the University, one of the smartest of the smart. I don't think MIT wants me taking up any of your cycles. In fact, I'm probably not allowed to."

"You are not a student," she said. "You are a worker."

"But you don't know me," I said, truly sounding like a student, the one with the dog and no homework.

Her hand moved on my arm.

"Professor Weingold has told me of you," she said. "You did not work hard in school. You had too many good times. Now I also want to have good times."

"Yikes."

She pointed at the building.

"Park in back," she said. "There is an assigned space for me there."

Liesl came up to my shoulder but there was no question who was in charge. I parked in back. She opened the door on the passenger's side and got out. I followed her to the back door of her building and up the stairs inside to the third floor, brushing raindrops out of my hair. She pulled out a key and stuck it in the lock.

"The school gives me this apartment for the semester." she said, opening the door. "It is too big."

The apartment was a flat that occupied the complete third floor. A hallway ran its length. Liesl took off her shoes and I followed suit. She pulled on slippers and handed me a pair. We padded down the hall. There were framed photos on the walls but in the gloom of day's end, the figures in them were swaddled in shadow. We passed a bedroom, a guest room, a room with a server rack and electronic equipment in it, a kitchen and dining room. The dining room table was set for two, with unlit candles and an empty vase.

Past a front stairwell, we entered a living room that spanned the width of the building. It was populated with two minimalist plank couches, a rattan coffee table, glass end tables with lamps in the shape of carved rabbits, a nickel swing-arm floor lamp, an empty birdcage, and an overhead light in a paper globe. Ancient Persian rugs covered most of the finished oak floor.

"This is American style?" the doctor said, patting one of the rabbits.

"A mixed bag."

She took out her phone and repeated my words into it. A female voice responded in German.

"Translation?" I said.

She nodded.

I helped her out of her raincoat, peeled off my jacket, and hung both on a coat rack standing inside the front door. I stepped back into the living room. Two canted bay windows overlooked Washington Street wet and shining as the street lights took hold in gray twilight. Rain rattled on the window panes.

The doctor disappeared down the hall. I switched on one of the lamps and perched on the edge of a couch. My reflection in the window stared back at me as the day failed.

The doctor returned wearing blue jeans and a sweatshirt with German script across its front. She carried a bottle and two glasses, which she arranged on the coffee table. She sat down beside me.

"Himbeergeist," she said. "It is raspberry schnapps. This is okay?"

"Sure," I said, although if I had ever tasted schnapps, I was too drunk at the time to remember.

This whole situation was as new to me as the schnapps.

She poured and we toasted each other.

"To a good semester," I said.

"To our friendship," she said.

Her cheeks glowed. I couldn't feel their heat from where I sat, but I wanted to.

"Doctor, listen, I..."

She held up a hand.

"For you, I am Liesl," she said. "You do not mind that I spoke to Professor Weingold about you?"

I shook my head.

"The school threw me out on my ear," I said. "Professor Weingold used to play poker with some of the IT guys. I did too. Instead of studying, I'd go over to Fenway Park or the Garden with them. Weingold warned me more than once that I was in trouble but it didn't help. I almost made it through, though."

Liesl lifted her glass again.

"Listen, Dr. Blau," I said. "I don't know how they do things in Germany, but I don't want to lose my job."

"Please say my name. Liesl. You will not lose your job."

An old-fashioned doorbell sounded in the hall. Liesl got up and buzzed the downstairs door open.

Galoshes clomped on the stairs. She opened the front door and greeted the delivery man standing there. She accepted a large paper bag and a bouquet of flowers, handed him a tip, thanked him, and closed the door.

"I do not cook," she said to me. "The University delivers dinner for me when I am home in the evening. Many nights I lecture. Tonight they have delivered dinner for two. The chefs at the Faculty Club prepared it."

She disappeared down the hall again, presumably to put the flowers in the empty vase and to do something with the food. When she returned and sat down beside me on the couch, her thigh pressed against mine. On its own, mine pressed back. My glass was empty.

"Now we eat dinner," Liesl said.

The bag from the Faculty Club sat on the dining room table. The flowers stood in water in the vase. We unpacked a green-bean-and-potato soup, rolled-up beef, bacon and onions, and potato dumplings and red cabbage. I opened a bottle of German red wine that came with the food.

"A German dinner," Liesl said.

She lit the candles and turned the lights lower and we sat down across from each other.

The setting had the feel of a state dinner. There was something very odd about the way the professor was interacting with me, beyond the basic miracle of her inviting me up in the first place. Odder than odd.

"I will stay until Christmas and go home," she said. This was in early September. "Where is your home?"

I told her about my youth in Los Angeles, my parents in Thousand Oaks, my brother in San Diego, my sister in Torrance.

"I did not go to school until the Institute accepted me," Liesl said. "We moved to the city from the country. The tutors came to my home when I was young. I studied science and mathematics. I learned to play the violin."

Her eyes seemed even wider than before, as if her words had carried her a step beyond theory. I swallowed some wine. She put her napkin to her lips.

"You will stay with me tonight?" she said.

She waited for me to respond without moving, but breathing quickly.

"Is this how they do it in Germany?" I said, feeling stupid as soon as I said it. A simple yes was beyond me. "Is this a good idea?"

"I do not know how they do it in Germany. This is not an idea. It is a desire."

My ears felt as red as the cabbage. I nodded. We got through dinner and left the dishes for the cleaning person sent over weekday mornings.

In bed, Liesl was precise and eager, then just eager, and then Mother Nature took over for both of us.

I was the teacher but she was the professor. We began with the lights out but turned them on again. There were periods of sleep, but not many. The rain fell through the night. By the time day dawned gray and still, we were groggy and laughing and horsing around like long-time lovers. We showered together and ate leftovers in bed.

We left the Jeep where I had parked it. The rain had let up and we walked to school on foot. Pigeons skirted puddles on the wet streets. A gentle breeze rustled damp autumn leaves on the trees we passed.

"Tonight I have a seminar until seven," Liesl said. "You will meet me in the Ayasli Conference Room after?"

I put my arm around her. She moved closer to me.

We walked down Windsor Street, out of the neighborhood and between four-story brick buildings to Mass Ave, crossing to the Flour Bakery for coffee and croissants. Stares meant for Dr. Blau grazed me. I was the curiosity sitting next to the celebrity.

"I have not had this thing in my life," Liesl said.

"This thing?"

"The touching," she said.

"Every night can't be like last night," I said.

She smiled. Her smile contained no hint of doubt or distrust, but something Delphic.

"We will see tonight," she said.

Back at school, I put off my coworkers' questions, which did not stop coming, and spent the day waiting for night.

And under the acacia tree in my Jeep, the Big Mac settled into my stomach and left me ready for the rest of the day's work, no co-workers involved.

Two weeks later, I was sitting in The Studio after work with a beer and bowl of pretzels in front of me. Four old sots swapped lies and kept me company at the bar. Walt was nodding on his stool by a metal sink full of pilsner glasses. A soccer game between two Mexican clubs unreeled in silence on the flatscreen.

"Go home, Dad," Mimi said, giving Walt a pat on the back. She came down the bar to the five of us.

"How are your seniors?" she said to me.

"Surprised by age."

"Would my dad fit in over there, when I finally get him to sell this place and retire?"

"The ladies will be all over him."

She glanced back at him on his stool.

"The centers aren't so different from this place," I said.

A hard guy in his fifties stepped into the bar, encased in a suit tailored for a bank president. He looked us over.

"Nice suit," I said.

"You making fun of it?" the guy said.

"Why? It's not yours?"

I was on my third beer with several shots of well gin thrown in. Mimi reached out and tapped my hand.

"I feel like a clown when I wear it," the guy said. "Cost enough for five suits."

"You get a promotion?" I said.

"Yeah. I'm a businessman now."

"If you say so."

He came over to the bar and gave me the look. Mimi tapped me again. The guy waved her off.

"I'm Tony Garza," he said to me. "Thanks for helping my mom the other day."

"Valeria. Nice lady. You're welcome."

"My daughter can get a little wild."

"Yeah," I said. "Racquetball, dinner with a guy, quiet party in Los Feliz."

"My mom is old-school. When my daughter goes out, her grandma fears the worst. Julieta is seventeen and she and Tommy Link are a thing, but that don't mean she can worry her grandma. I like Tommy, but a guy's a guy, you know what I mean? Julieta should've checked before she took off like that. It's a rule."

"You want something to drink?"

Mimi drifted back. The geezers shifted down the bar, giving us room.

"Johnny Walker Blue," Garza said to her. "Bring over the bottle."

"No black, gold, platinum, or blue in this joint," Mimi said. "You're lucky to get red."

"Do I know you?" Garza said to her.

"I'm Mimi. Walt's kid."

"You know Julieta? She went to East Valley."

"I knew her big sister Mariana."

"So what about this guy here? He dependable?"

"The old folks love him."

"What's your opinion?"

She shrugged.

"He's sitting here half-drunk," she said. "What does that tell you?"

She fetched the bottle of Johnny Red and sat it on the bar, along with a tumbler for Garza and a couple of bar napkins. I swallowed the last of the beer in my glass and slid it over next to the tumbler. Garza poured out a dose for each of us, ignoring the foam remnants in my glass.

"Nothing to drink worthy of that suit in this dive," I said to Garza.

He looked down and ran a palm over the fine material of the suit coat. His calluses produced a scratching sound.

"You asked if I got promoted," he said. "Yeah. I've been in collections for years. Now I'm in charge of loans."

"You don't look too happy about it."

"I'm not so good with numbers. I'm not so good at giving orders. I'm not so good at knowing who to give money to and when to say no. Collecting, I'm good at."

"So why the promotion?"

"My boss got... got fired. The head of the company decided to try me out. He says I'm trustworthy. My boss wasn't."

"You could've said no."

"Uh huh," he said, meaning nuh uh. "Anyway, I'm here now because I'm looking for Tommy Link and my daughter won't tell me where he is. We were arguing about it and my mom reminded me how quick you found my daughter last week. My mom says I should ask you to find Tommy the same way. She says Julieta might be tweeting at him or texting him or whatever the hell they do these days and you could spot him on your computer."

He pulled out a packet of hundred-dollar bills and handed it to me. I laid it on the bar. Down the bar, Jorge Gonzalez got up like the money was a signal and headed out. Freddie and Juan moved to the pool table. Hoang limped to the bathroom.

"I got lucky finding Julieta," I said. "I'd never find Tommy."

"My mom says you'll find him. He's popular in the Valley. If you don't find him in LA, check Reno and Vegas. He gambles. Go home and use your computer. What are you doing in a joint like this anyway?"

"It's not home but it sort of feels like it," I said.

Garza had the shoulders of a lineman. He loomed. A powerful guy, like an ox is powerful. I had an idea, though, that in spite of his ox-like strength, his mom, wife, and daughter probably shared the reins to his yoke.

"If finding my daughter was luck, good for you," he said. "Now you can be lucky some more."

The hands sticking out of his suit looked like they could hurt somebody. I kept quiet. Instead of answering, I took a manly swallow.

Garza knocked back the liquid in his glass in an unsuitlike way.

"I help you find the guy, then what?" I said.

He pointed at the hundreds.

"I mean, to Tommy," I said.

"Doesn't matter."

"Does to me."

"Doesn't to you. You find him, you get the finder's fee. Do what you do on the computer, however you do it, I don't care. Google him like you did my daughter."

"You said you didn't care, he took your daughter out. She didn't ask permission but is that Tommy's fault?"

"I like the kid. This isn't about my daughter."

"What's it about?"

"Money. He owes it."

"And can't pay it?"

"Why I can't find him."

"My gift for using the computer won't work if you're going to hurt this guy," I said. The alcohol fumes cleared off my brainpan for a minute, stirred by a puff from the winds of concern. "My gift comes from a good fairy, not a bad one."

"You sound like the fairy," Garza said. "I'm not going to hurt the kid."

I searched his face and couldn't find a lie hiding there, but that's because it was hiding.

"Work with me, Tony," I said.

Garza sighed. He seemed like a calm guy, but there was nothing calming about him. I didn't want him angry. I didn't want him taking off his suit coat to keep the blood from splashing on it. I suspected blood was not unusual in his line of work, at least before he got promoted.

"You like to haggle, huh, Saul? Get the best deal?"

"Are you talking about my nose?"

Hoang came back from the bathroom and stood watching the other two at the pool table. The soccer match continued in silence. A guy I didn't know dozed over his beer at a table in the back.

"I'm not trying to make a deal," I said. "I don't want some kid's blood on my hands."

"I promised my daughter I wouldn't kill him or cripple him."

"You said you're not in collections anymore. Somebody else going to collect from Tommy?"

"I'm handling this one personally," Garza said.

I didn't have to think long about that one.

"You loaned him the money and you want to clean this up quietly," I said.

"The organization is gonna take the money from me when they find out. Nothing I can do about that, but if I don't work the boy over, they're gonna work me over instead."

"How much does Tommy owe?"

"Twenty large, plus the vig."

"Yow. How did that happen?"

"He's got a gambling problem."

"I mean, how did he get into you for that much?"

"I'm new at making loans instead of collecting on them. Tommy scores big sometimes. He knows sports. He's an excellent poker player. Also, his father is rich. Only lately Tommy isn't doing so good. He's taken some real bad beats at the table. He keeps explaining how he's due to bounce back. He's a convincing kid. Also my daughter leaned on me a little. I thought his father would bail him out. I called the old man when Tommy couldn't pay up. I got the horse laugh. His old man told me Tommy was kicked out of UCLA for organizing poker games in the dorm. The family disowned him."

I finished my Red. Garza made no move to refill either glass. I sensed he was done drinking.

"You're the new guy in charge of loans," I said, "and the first thing, you let a kid take you for a ride."

He tightened up at that but his suit and new responsibilities reined him in.

"Yeah," he said. "Like I told you, I don't make an example out of him, somebody is gonna make an example out of me."

I pushed my glass away.

"It's nothing personal," he said. "He told me he had a sure thing. I'm the sucker here. He promised me if he won the bet, he'd pay me off and use the rest of the money to check into a treatment program. He told me he was already going to Gamblers Anonymous. Probably a line, but the kid sold me on it. Maybe he sold himself and Julieta too. In spite of everything, I like Tommy."

"So I helped your mother find your daughter and now I'm supposed to help you find Tommy so you can beat him up?"

A cloud passed over his face.

"I promised my daughter about Tommy," he said. "I didn't make any promises about you."

"How would your mom like it, you hurt me?"

"My mom knows the business. I'm a pussycat compared to what my dad was. She knows it's never personal with me."

He let me sweat a minute and then poked me in the chest.

"I'm messing with you," he said. "Turn me down and the worst I'll do is send somebody over to bust up that damned computer of yours."

All of a sudden the bar came into focus.

"What if I can't find him?" I said.

"My mom says if you look, you'll find. Tommy stands out. He can't help it. He's got to be a player, if not here, then somewhere else."

"You haven't found him."

"He's staying clear of the books and casinos around here. If he's gambling online or he's left town, you're the guy to figure it out."

"Tommy Link," I said.

"Tommy Link. Where're you from, anyway?"

"I grew up in Thousand Oaks. Then I went back east for a while."

"What are you doing in this neighborhood?"

"Close to my job. When did you last see Mr. Link?"

"When I gave him his final warning Sunday night. One more day to bring me the money."

"Who else have you got after him?" I said.

"Nobody. I want to keep this quiet. I've put the word out a little bit, but my collection guys aren't working on it."

"Where did you talk to Tommy last Sunday?"

"The Dot."

"Over on Victory?" I said. "What time?"

"Maybe ten, ten-thirty that night."

"What does Tommy look like?"

I already knew, of course, but I wanted to make an impression.

"Nice clean kid. Grew up in Canoga Park. Tall. Blond hair. Used to wear an expression said he knew it all. That was before this losing streak. Now he's hangdog."

"And what would the example look like, if you made one out of him?"

"It would look like somebody would say, what the hell happened to him? He'd still be walking, though, at least after a while."

"Come back tomorrow night," I said.

Garza pulled out a pen and wrote a phone number on a napkin. He pushed it over to me and stood up. The money remained where it was.

"You'll get a bonus for finding Tommy quick, like you found my daughter," he said. "Call me when you do, or I'll be here tomorrow night. Ten o'clock."

He shook the wrinkles out of his trousers. Mimi came over to reclaim the Johnny Walker and glasses.

"Say hello to Mariana for me," she said to Garza.

He nodded and walked out.

Mimi eyed the hundreds lying on the bar.

"That's not good," she said.

"He wants some computer help."

"Yeah? My advice, don't give it."

"He was persuasive," I said.

Mimi yawned and pushed her hair behind her ears.

"One more hit?" I said, picking up my glass.

"You've had enough. You going to help him?"

"He said he'd smash my computer."

"They say things like that. It's part of the business."

"He won't smash it?"

"No, he'll smash it. He just won't enjoy smashing it."

I groaned.

"I can't find a kid he's going to hurt," I said. "How did I get into this?"

"Tell him you tried and couldn't find him."

"If I try, I'll find him. I'm afraid to lie to this guy. Not when I'm sober."

"Are you sober now?"

"I'm not drunk enough, that's for sure."

"Stall him," Mimi said. "Maybe he'll find the boyfriend in the meantime."

My glass was still in my hand. I held it out. She sighed and poured a finger into it.

"Let's pray the kid is long gone," I said.

"When is Tony coming back?"

"Tomorrow night. Here."

"He wants to put this to bed," Mimi said.

I stood up, stuffed the money in my pocket, and drained my glass.

"Good night, guys," I said to the trio at the pool table.

They dropped their cues on the green baize and returned to the bar. I ignored their questioning looks and took an egg from the basket on the bar. Mimi cleared my glass.

Outside, Magnolia was quiet but LA's white noise, the sound of a gigantic but distant engine, stood in as windsong. Jekell and Bush were camped out on the sidewalk, along with a friend named Jesse. I gave Jekell and Jesse five bucks each and Bush his egg.

The alcohol put a little air under my feet. I left the Jeep on the curb and walked home on pillowy sidewalks. A breeze as soft as the pavement ruffled my hair. Streetlights buzzed, covering the city's lullaby and mingling with a buzz growing inside my head. I pushed away thoughts of Garza. The secret of the scanner was not in danger. I could locate Tommy and then quit performing insignificant acts of good will, finding cats, parakeets, and granddaughters. The buzz in my head was probably my conscience.

Liesl wasted no time introducing me to the scanner. While I waited for her in 6B the second night, outside the conference room, emotions roamed from my brain to my heart to points south, fogging over any lurking doubts. One night with Liesl and I was full of irrational, one-sided love.

We walked back to the apartment talking about professors Zhang and Bogolubov, two contentious characters bent on bringing Liesl to heel. Instead they ended up bowing to her arguments and conceding the evening to her. I was in semi-possession of my wits again after our night together, but the skeptical, pessimistic side of my spirit remained quiet with Liesl occasionally bumping me from the side as we walked. The Cambridge neighborhood had become an enchanted kingdom.

Our catered dinner arrived and after we ate, Liesl led me to the room with the electronics equipment in it and flipped the light switch. A 42U server rack stood against the back wall with a single blade server installed in it. Next to the rack sat a unit the size of a mini fridge.

My thoughts, unlike my body, were located in the next room down the hall.

Cables ran from the server and boxy unit to a console sitting on a deal table in the middle of the room. A keyboard, two wireless VR headsets and a multifunction game controller rested next to the console. There were no add-on controllers that could be latched to the hands, so the device was designed for watching, not moving. The VR equipment looked hybridized but larger and more impressive than anything I had ever used.

"What's this?" I said.

"I will show you."

"Can the wiring in this old house handle the load?"

"Not so much power is needed."

The curtains were drawn. Liesl pushed a button that powered up the system.

We walked over to the table and sat down in office chairs in front of the console. The controller on the table was far more complicated than any I had ever seen.

"I built it," Liesl said, indicating the equipment.

"What is it?"

"A scanner," she said. "The word is the same in German."

"What does it scan?"

"I have thought about how to explain this."

"Yes?"

"It is better to show you."

I was thinking about the previous night and the night to come, not about headsets and joysticks. I tried to pay attention.

"I will show you," she repeated.

She noticed the impatient look on my face and poked my stomach.

"It is important to me," she said.

"I'm sorry," I said. Her poke did the trick. My thoughts returned from the bedroom to us.

She picked up a headset and strapped it on. She settled the controller in her lap.

"I will operate the device," she said. "Put on your headset, please."

I pulled it on and spent a minute tightening its straps to fit me. With both of us ready, I heard a rattle of keys and a click and a 3D virtual-reality scene phased in around me. I was looking at the room from above and behind us, as if suspended from the ceiling. I turned my head. The room's windows on the east side were behind me. The overhead light was on my right, at eye level. The clarity of the optics was amazing. Unbelievable, actually, compared to the VR systems I had tried, some of which were state-of-the-art examples available at the University.

"This is real virtual," I said.

"Tell me what you want to see."

"What do you mean?"

"From anywhere in the world. From the past or the future."

"Dinosaurs?" I said, to humor her.

"Dinosaurs. Of course."

"Too easy?" I said.

A click and I was sitting on a sunny plain with green fronds up to my chin. In front of me grazed a herd of dinosaurs I didn't recognize.

"One hundred million years ago," Liesl said. Her voice came to me from my left but she wasn't in the image.

"Wow," I said.

"Choose something else," she said.

"You choose."

A pause and a click and I was in the midst of a small crowd on a muddy street listening to Abraham Lincoln give a stump speech.

Another pause and click and I was standing on the moon looking up at the Earth.

A final click and the headset went dark. I pulled it off.

"This technology is the ultimate," I said. "It's incredible. Beyond words. Beyond immersive. You are about to revolutionize the media world forever. What about action? Avatars? What about building characters online? You can buy VR property online, you know…"

"I will teach you to use it," Liesl said.

"How many scenarios like that have you got?"

"More than you will watch," she said. She was gazing at me.

"What?" I said, and after a moment's thought, "Why me?"

"I have not showed the scanner to anyone. I think you will enjoy it. I will answer all your questions after you use it. Now it is time for bed."

I was distracted a little at first, in the other room, but it didn't last.

And now I sat alone in the night in North Hollywood with a bottle of scotch and the scanner, but no Liesl.

With time in reverse, I followed myself back to Garza at the bar and tracked him into the past, back to The Dot Lounge on Sunday night. I switched to time-forward when he braced Tommy at a table by the front window. Tommy was sitting with friends. He was a good-looking kid, but he had a worried expression on his face. He was too young to be in the bar, not that The Dot was famous for carding its customers.

All conversation ceased when Garza stepped up to the table. He leaned over and said a few words to Tommy. I could read lips a little, but not Garza's at that angle. I moved around in front of him and backed up a few seconds and let Garza say it again.

"You've got a day."

Tommy nodded. Garza left. I stuck with Tommy. He said a word or two to the others, waiting for Garza to get clear, and then left himself. Outside he climbed into his Cutlass and drove over to an apartment on Archwood, just off Lankershim.

I followed him in. He threw some clothes into a duffle. Stuffed a toiletry kit, a fresh deck of cards and a pillow into a backpack, and back out he went.

He got behind the wheel and hauled ass out of North Hollywood, jumping on the Ventura Freeway heading east to its terminus in Pasadena, where he continued onto the 210. He got off in East Pasadena and made his way over to a bungalow on Backus Avenue. I bookmarked the location on the scanner.

Tommy was out of North Hollywood but not out of town.

An old woman let him in when he knocked. I turned up the scan rate. In minutes the sun came up Monday morning and Tommy emerged, clothes unchanged. I followed him around the Valley for three days, doing a fast scan most of the way. He drove from place to place, borrowing money or trying to. He scored a couple of times from men he knew, but no one fronted him serious cash. He collected enough to lay a bet or two but nothing that would save him from Garza. He sat in on a couple of poker games but played tight and tilted, like a guy weighed down. Tuesday morning he stopped in Reseda and bought a fake beard.

After two hours of scanning and a concomitant amount of scotch, Tommy and I reached Wednesday night, at which time he picked up Julieta at Westfield Fashion Square in Sherman Oaks. Together they drove to central Los Angeles and attended another Gamblers Anonymous meeting, this time as a couple, at the church in Koreatown.

This kid was not leaving LA. At first I wondered if he knew what was in store for him if he stayed, but after seeing the troubled expression remain unchanged on his face for three days, I knew that he knew.

I skipped the rest of Wednesday night and jumped ahead to eight o'clock this morning, back at the bungalow on Backus. I goosed the scan rate and Tommy emerged at eleven-thirty wearing the fake beard, sunglasses, and a straw hat. He drove over to the Santa Anita race track three miles east of the bungalow and parked in the Gate 8 lot.

I followed him in. He bought a general admission ticket and a copy of the day's Racing Form. He walked directly to the paddock. I was surprised at the size of the crowd, given racing's downward spiral. Perhaps the warm May day brought everyone out, or perhaps this was the season's first day. I hadn't been to the track since high school.

Tommy took up a position near the Seabiscuit statue and studied his paper, waiting for the horses to be led past to the saddling barn. He wasn't trying to hide. He had more confidence in his disguise than I did. It attracted curious children.

After observing the horses parade for the first race, he followed them out to the track and took a seat in the grandstand to watch them warm up. Eventually they headed at a walk toward the starting gate and Tommy went in to the betting windows and stood in line to place his first bets of the day, instead of keeping his head down and using his phone or a machine teller. Reckless.

It was twelve-thirty.

I zoomed in to check out his play at the window. His bets were of the exotic variety. He boxed three horses for the Trifecta, betting on the six possible combinations of Win, Place, and Show for the three horses of his choice. He bought a ten-dollar ticket for the Pick Six, which required him to name the winners of six races in a row. He was trying to pick winners in cheap claiming races. A magic eight ball would help him as much as his Racing Form.

Back in the grandstand, he watched the first race. When it was over, he tore up his tickets.

Exotic bets can pay off in the thousands on a good day, but only because the odds of winning with them are long, longer, and forget about it. I was no expert but I had put in some hooky time at Santa Anita and at Suffolk Downs in East Boston. I knew a parlay from a paddock.

Tommy spent the rest of the day attempting to win the money he needed to keep his face and limbs in their present condition. From what I saw, he didn't win enough to save an eyelash, never mind his nose, his teeth, or his life.

I was numb by then. The night felt a thousand years old and so did I. I hurried through the next eight races. How long could the boy hang out there without being spotted by some railbird who'd drop a dime on him with a call to Garza?

He spoke to no one. Neither Garza nor the goons Garza undoubtedly employed descended upon him, but Tommy would not get out from under the man this way.

The last race went off at 4:41 in the afternoon. I left Johnny sitting in the grandstand with a blank look on the visible portions of his face. Part of the money he had scrounged during the week now belonged to the track. After a day's work, all he had was another tale of woe for his friends at Gamblers Anonymous.

He finally bestirred himself and trudged back to his car. He drove to the bungalow, parked in the street, and went inside. I bid him good night.

I powered down the scanner, stood up, took three steps to the easy chair by the door. I had rescued this castoff from the curbside in Van Nuys. I fell into it and took a breath. Tired but okay. Good. I was still able to think. Not good. But sleep solved that.

~~~

The morning after Liesl unveiled her scanner, we got up tired but satisfied. The scanner ran a distant second in my thoughts, amazing as it was.

We walked to school again, heading back to the bakery first. The morning was temperate, the puddles had shrunk, and students were afoot.

"I did not tell you something last night," Liesl said.

"Yes?"

"Yesterday I asked John Martins to lend you to me for the semester."

"The head of IS&T? What did he say?"

"Of course he said yes."

"What did you have in mind?"

"If we are to spend this time together, I am asking you to plan it for us, the time when I am free from seminars and lectures."

"I can do that," I said.

We strolled along the sidewalk toward Mass Ave, the occasional dog yapping at us from behind a fence.

"What about that scanner?" I said. "Are you going to sell it? How does it work?"

"I will teach you to use the scanner. After you learn, I will explain how it works."

"Why keep it a secret from others? Why show it to me?"

"First you will use it and then I will explain it."

"But..."

"First you will use it"

First I would use it.

A young man with a Harvard book bag ventured to nod to us as we all waited to cross Main Street. Liesl paid him no mind.

"Where do you live?" she said to me.

"Somerville. I have a studio apartment near Powderhouse Square."

"Perhaps you will go there and gather your clothes and bring them to my apartment."

"Perhaps so."

Our two nights together made this seem most natural.

"Everyone is talking about your theories," I said. She nodded.

"Can you give me a layman's summary? The thirty-thousand-foot view?"

"Of course," she said, and without my realizing it, began to outline for me the theory behind her scanner.

"The most important principle is that there are more than three dimensions," she said.

"Ten or so, seven of them curled up? String theory?"

Her lips firmed up as she suppressed a smile. I made a mental note never to say anything about physics around her again.

"An infinite number," she said. "Not curled up."

"Wait. When you say dimension..."

"A measurable extent," she said. "Our organs of sense perceive three of them. Evolution made this choice. The Euclidean three-manifolds. The state-space of quantum mechanics, an infinite-dimensional function space. You understand dimensions in this way?"

"I know one when I see one."

"Now assume that any two points in space are contiguous in some dimension," she said, ignoring my whimsy or unfamiliar with the expression.

"Every point in the universe touches every other point?"

"A pin through crumpled paper," she said. "Every point in our first-order multiverse touches all other points in the multiverse."

"It's adding up," I said.

This got me a look of surmise.

"What about time?" I said. "That's a dimension too, isn't it?"

"Time is not a dimension. Time's flow is variable and the arrow of time points in a different direction for every physical dimension."

"Not for our three. Time runs the same way in our three."

We both hopped to the right on the sidewalk as a car splashed through a puddle in the street beside us.

"No," Liesl said. "Evolution chose three dimensions with arrows almost parallel. The difference between them will not be evident for billions of years. Then causality will become confusing."

"It's already become confusing," I said. "I don't understand your model, but I intuit an environment of extreme shear."

"Ignore multidimensional causality and all is simple," Liesl said, "if you are able to create the new mathematical techniques necessary to calculate predictive behavior for any subset of these orthogonal dimensions. The arrows of time are not orthogonal in any sense. There is no absolute past or future. Each arrow defines the past and future for one dimension. Matter and energy do not care."

"Keep in mind that I flunked out," I said.

"You were lazy but you are not stupid."

"So every particle of matter in my body exists in an infinity of dimensions? With time running across the multiverse in a different direction for each dimension of each particle, while touching every point in the universe in the next Planck unit of time simultaneously?"

Liesl nodded.

"And when you add it up, this is it?" I said and spread my arms.

"We perceive only the smallest bit of what this is," she said, passing her hand back and forth in the air as we walked.

"So I'm getting older, younger, and everything in between simultaneously?"

"Yes," she said, and chucked me on the arm.

"The complexity is insane."

"Consider it turbulence."

Four blocks remained between us and muffins and coffee. We spent the time deciding what to do the coming evening, a task that would occupy me a great deal for the next three months.

After my evening scanning Tommy's week, I woke up Friday morning with my head banging. I had the sweats as I shaved and showered and dressed and drove over to Hesby Seniors.

I took an ibuprofen 800 and poured a cup of black coffee in the center's office, a distressed laptop waiting for me on the desk. A taxi pulled up outside and Cannelita Bertoni got out. She spotted me when she came in, and angled over to the office.

"You okay?" she said.

"Sure," I said. "Why do you ask?"

"You're a drinker."

"Who says?"

"I was married to one for forty years."

"What's up, Cannelita?"

"I just got off the phone with Valeria Garza, over at Lankershim. She told me about how you found her granddaughter. She also told me about a cat you found recently. You're a miracle worker according to her."

"I'm here to help with the computers, Cannelita. I've got a lot on my mind."

"Drink the coffee, Saul. It'll help. Do you smoke? Smoking helps."

"I don't smoke."

"Eat something greasy."

"You throwing your money away on taxis now?" I said.

"I came in a taxi because I can't find my car key and I don't know how to get ahold of the Uber guys. I've been looking for the key since last night. I'm at my wit's end."

I stared at her.

"And?" I said.

"I want you to find it. You're the one can find things."

"Oh my God," I said. "Really?"

"I took my granddaughters to the movies and out for ice cream last night. After, I drove them back to their place and talked to my daughter for a while. When I got home, I locked the car with the key. I heard the beep. Later I wanted to get back into the car for a drawing one of my granddaughters did while I was talking to her mom and I couldn't find the key."

She stood there with an expectant look on her face.

"When I'm done here, I'll give you a ride home," I said. "We'll retrace your steps and find the key... Just a single key?"

"I hide my house key in my yard so I won't lose it. Look, just find my car key now, on that," she said, pointing at the computer. "You don't need to make a special trip."

"I'm saving you the cab fare," I said.

Cannelita nodded and headed off to her Peace of Mind class in the San Fernando room. I sat waiting for my pill to kick in. Another satisfied customer. I could satisfy Garza too, without Tommy getting hurt, but it meant helping Tommy make some money and I wasn't crazy about doing that.

My third evening with Liesl, I went over to the school and we walked back to her apartment together, freshened up, and took the T over to Boston's North End. We had a look at the Old North Church and dinner at a lively, no-frills Italian place on Hanover Street. I used my phone and we caught a quick lift to a club off Boylston across from the Boston Common. The line moved fast. Liesl got checked with rigor because she looked so young. She got in free, as we had arrived a little early in the evening. Inside, the bouncers had all got word of her Aryan aspect and accent and being white-power types, made sure to come over, get acquainted with her and assure her that she'd have a good time. I was invisible to them.

In no time we had a premium table and sat drinking and watching the DJ in action. The drinks were weak, a good thing, and the music had a West Coast feel. The bouncers stayed close. Liesl handled them like she handled her students.

"There are these types everywhere," she said to me, not in a harsh way, indicating the nearest of them.

"No problem for you," I said.

She seemed to enjoy the music and the scene. I knew the DJ and introduced her to him, and to some kids from BU. We tried a little dancing. Liesl kept it simple but put out a European vibe that drew frequent looks. The security team kept hopeful eyes on her, ready to come over for any reason.

On the way back to Cambridge, we held hands sitting side by side in a subway car on the Blue Line. I had done some hand-holding in my time, but never like this. I was out of my depth, out of my league, and a little out of my mind.

In the morning, Liesl sat me down in front of the scanner and after powering on the console but not the scanner, explained the controller to me in detail, displaying a generous list of commands on the console screen. Afterwards, we walked down for breakfast and over to the campus. We parted at Liesl's office door and I found myself free for the day and returned to the flat and the scanner.

It did not take me long to master the system's controls, given Liesl's training that morning. In an hour or two I could go where I wanted, in time, in physical location, in whatever universe. It also did not take me long to realize that I was not dealing with a video game or any other VR product-to-be. When I could no longer deny the truth, I stopped scanning, unstrapped my headset, and left the room to pace around the apartment.

When I first powered up the system I had focused on the virtual me and had put time in reverse. I watched myself back up through the morning, increasing the scan or framing rate. In minutes I was following myself back through the past days, then weeks. I stopped the scan, shaking my head and muttering to myself, reset the device to the present moment and scanned across adjacent worlds in the multiverse. I passed over a monumental number of them before the image of me in the room changed. I was sitting in a different position. Again I increased the scan rate by orders of magnitude, until the other me was dressed differently than I was, then no longer in the room. Then the room was gone. I stepped up the rate again and eventually the Earth itself was gone.

I stopped the scan and reset the device. I almost quit then but forced myself to do a third scan. I kept time and the universe constant and scanned up into space. In spite of the knowledge that I was sitting in a room in Cambridge, my stomach did a few flip-flops as I gained altitude. I didn't bother with the solar system, increasing the scan rate for space, not time, and zooming right into the center of the galaxy where I cut the engines, so to speak, and sat staring at the supermassive black hole in front of me. It wasn't eating a star at the moment. Thank God for the conservation of angular momentum or we'd all be inside the thing by now. Its event horizon shone with a peculiar light. I thought about scanning right into it, but I wasn't ready for that.

I navigated up along the galaxy's axis of rotation until I had a view of the whole barred, multi-armed spiral, two hundred billion stars glowing below me. When my thumb discontinued the scan with a click, two hours had passed and I was disoriented and had trouble standing up.

I powered down the system and retrieved a beer from the fridge, pacing the apartment as I drank it. I reviewed Liesl's little science talk about dimensions.

I drank a second beer in front of the console. My gaze kept returning to the future toggle on the controller. I reached for my headset twice but didn't pull it on. When the beer was gone, I got up, went downstairs, jumped in the Jeep, and drove over to Somerville to collect my clothes and some toiletries. My landlady asked me where I had been. I gave her a hug but words failed me and I left her standing on the stoop. From there I drove over to a cafe and bar named Cabhan's, two blocks off Inman Square.

On Thursdays, Cabhan's rolled out the corned beef and cabbage on paper plates at happy hour. Alcoholic graduate students used the occasion to eat, drink and avoid their studies.

I arrived before that, at three in the afternoon. A Boston Irish guy named Brian kept the bar weekdays between lunch and dinner. He set me up without asking.

"If you had a chance to know the future, would you go for it?" I said to him. Every other customer in the place was on a phone or tablet or reading an old-fashioned book.

"I know the future already," he said.

"Yeah?"

"The kids are almost grown. Me and the old lady are getting older. Pretty soon we'll be grandma and grandpa and after that, you know, the lights go out."

"Jesus," I said.

I threw back the shot and he gave me another. When Liesl walked home alone after school that night, she found me asleep on one of the couches. I apologized and began to explain.

"Do not worry," she said. "This will not be a problem for us."

"You know that," I said, "because you checked the future."

"For me, the past is not important. The future is important. It has been my true university."

"Don't tell me what happens," I said.

She didn't.

"Is this why you want to spend a semester here exploring life instead of doing research? Something bad is going to happen?"

The doorbell rang. She stood up.

"Well?" I said.

"Do you want to know?"

"No. Yes. I don't know. Do I? Is it bad news?"

She let me think about that while she buzzed in the delivery boy.

"One semester and that's it?" I said.

I heard our dinner coming up the stairs.

"Don't tell me," I said. "I don't want to know."

In the following weeks, while Liesl was lecturing or leading a seminar, I used the scanner. The University was happy, not to say enthralled, with her. She was queen of the campus. My friends in IT tried to corner me, desperate for the lowdown, but I has been snatched from them by the object of their interest.

She asked me why in particular I avoided the future. I told her that for me, the future was the last chapter in every book, the final standings for every season, the mother of all spoilers. The future featured the bad news, the worst news, the news we try to ignore, the death news.

I settled in as Liesl's roommate, tour guide, and lover. I planned our nights out and our weekend excursions. We visited Walden Pond, where I read Thoreau to her while we picnicked. I took her to the USS Constitution, Faneuil Hall, and other such historical spots. We paddled a rowboat on the Assabet river, keeping our fingers out of the water because of the snapping turtles. A mink swam beside us, just beyond my left oar.

I called a scalper I knew and we took the T to Kenmore Square and watched a Red Sox playoff game from the bleacher seats at Fenway. Professor Weingold shared his Celtics season tickets with us and we sat behind the team bench at the Garden. We dined out and hit some more dance clubs. Rode the T or a bus back home when I was too high to drive.

Liesl was consistently present and interested. She smiled a lot. Her smile reminded me of the weather, sometimes sunny, sometimes shadowed with a hint of winter. Her lips defined the non-toxic knowing smile. No matter how rowdy the venue, she was never treated with disrespect.

We took in the fall color in New Hampshire, caught the ferry to Martha's Vineyard, and rode the Acalea Express First Class twice to Penn Station and back, spending two weekends in Manhattan. We flew in a Cape Air Cessna 402 from Logan to Provincetown for a weekend on Cape Cod and drove to Niagara Falls one Friday, starting out at seven in the morning and arriving at a scenic lookout in the late afternoon.

With the scanner, meanwhile, I traveled a little farther than New York or Niagra.

In space, the scanner filtered the sun. Liesl had bookmarked the planets, so I wasn't the first to see them up close. I took exponential steps back to the center of the galaxy until I reached its black hole. Instead of stopping, this time I kept going. The scanner obliged me by stepping past the hole's event horizon and into its interior, where I found a meadow. I backed out with my eyes closed.

After that I stepped out beyond our galactic cluster, beyond our supercluster, beyond the Sloan Great Wall, searching for an end to existence or an edge or a curve that would bring me back home, or for any other boundary or limit to reality. I never found one and Liesl said that I never would.

The search wasn't boring but finally began to

seem pointless, then comical, then depressing. I ran time backwards to render the expanding universe smaller but I never made it small enough to find its limits, if it had any.

I did some moderate drinking during these sessions, but made sure that I was clear when Liesl got off in the evenings. Most of the time.

I found life amongst the stars to be pervasive but not profuse. Most planets not dead were dense with biomass. Nature would evolve a clever biological machine, like the ribosome on Earth, and elaborate it, improvising a planet full of life forms. The bands of similar worlds in the multiverse thinned when life was present on a world and thinned some more when that life was sentient, as choice replaced instinct.

I scanned sentient races but found none technologically superior to humans in any obvious way. Signs of extinct races argued variously for deadly cosmic events and killer technologies.

I scanned back in time to view the formation of the Earth. Stars crowded the night sky over our glowing planet, Sol still in the gas cloud that birthed it.

Without Liesl to scoff, I returned to the dinosaurs, two hundred million years of them. I browsed while they browsed. When some of them evolved feathers for warmth and then mating rituals, they became gaudy as peacocks.

The seas boiled with life. The land grew thick with it, matted with it, unlike today's worn planet.

I hopped to Washington for a scan of Lincoln when he was older than I had last seen him. Crossed the Earths in our band of the multiverse looking for a strip of them where Booth's weapon misfired. It took some time. Booth fumbled with the weapon and Lincoln popped him a good one.

"You don't use the scanner anymore," I said to Liesl once, early on. We were sitting on a boulder halfway up Mount Washington on a Saturday afternoon. She made a dismissive gesture.

The White Mountains were arrayed in ranks to the west under a gradient of low sky. The day was clear when we started up the trail, but a floor of clouds had materialized as we hiked along. Liesl took in the panorama spread out before us. A gaggle of birders passed while we rested, arguing about a recent sighting of the elusive migrating Bicknell's Thrush.

"You're famous for your theories," I said to Liesl. "Did you find them in the future?"

She stood up, gazing at the distant peaks. Her eyes were as gray as the clouds.

"Nichts ist wertvoller als dieser Tag," she said.

"Your phone is turned off."

"Nothing is worth more than this day," Liesl said. "It is a quote from Goethe. You cannot relive yesterday. Tomorrow is still beyond your reach."

Liesl knew things. Things I didn't know. Things I wasn't sure I wanted to know. She was embedded in life while I skated over its surface. I was drawn to her, excited and calmed by her, but most of all, in complete awe of her. She was visiting my world but didn't live in it.

"There are answers in the future," she said, "but not all the answers."

"The future goes all the way out, doesn't it?"

She raised an eyebrow. I bit my tongue.

Her hair was done up in some sort of strict German braid.

"I do not tell my colleagues everything," she said. "Some things I do not want them to know."

"Sufficient to the day is the evil thereof," I said,

quoting from the upstart testament.

It was time to start back. The weather, famously erratic on that mountain, was not to be trusted, especially when clouds were involved. We pulled on our packs.

"I will tell you everything if you ask," she said.

I kissed her and settled for that.

We stayed the night in the Redstone Lodge, in a room up top with slanted ceiling and dormer windows. At dinner I ventured to bring up the future again.

"I've been wondering," I said. "You scanned us a year ago when you were living in Germany. What you saw then is happening now, correct? Isn't that some sort of time loop?"

"The world has branched uncountable times since I scanned us."

"I know, but still. Maybe the Liesl on the world you were scanning scanned this world. That would be a loop involving two universes."

We were eating Jackson salad and New England chili in the lodge dining room. We were tired and hungry but satisfied with our day on the mountain. I had consumed a dirty martini and a glass of porter before the chili arrived.

"There are no loops," Liesl said.

"But after countless Liesls observe the future of countless other Liesls, aren't you eventually bound to end up with a loop somewhere?"

"No loops."

"Wouldn't you run out of Liesls? Wouldn't the final Liesl be forced to create a loop by scanning the future of one of the previous Liesls?"

"There are always more Liesls."

"Infinite Liesls? Isn't that a paradox in itself?"

"Infinities do not create paradoxes. They solve them."

A lot of our conversations ended like that. I was talking to an oracle crossed with a sphinx.

I gave Cannelita of the lost key her ride home late Friday afternoon. She lived on Kling Street, on the other side of the Ventura Freeway. Her home had a Fifties look to it, with a rough brick chimney stuck to the front of the house. The yard was landscaped in pebbles and overgrown drought-resistant plants. A large white cat with black and brown markings came out to greet us at the curb, tail up.

"Okay," I said to Cannelita when we got out of my Jeep. "Let's find your key."

Cannelita picked up the cat with an effort.

"That's a good-looking cat," I said. It studied me with blue eyes. "What kind is it?"

"She's a ragdoll. It's a newer breed. Very lovable. She follows me around like a little dog. Where's your computer?"

"Let's start the old-fashioned way," I said.

A Kia Rio was parked in the driveway. I walked over to the driver's side. The car was locked.

"You beeped it locked?" I said.

Cannelita nodded. I bent down and looked under the car. Nothing. I inspected the ice plant next to the car. No key. I followed the stone path that curved from the driveway around to the front porch. I rustled each bush, left and right, as I came to it, checking underneath.

"I did that already," Cannelita said. She cradled the cat in her arms.

"Did you go inside your house with the key?"

"No. I unlocked the front door with the house

key, but before I went in, I remembered that I had left my granddaughter's drawing in the car and I went back to get it, but I couldn't get in."

I came off the porch and walked back to the driver's side of the Kia. I motioned and Cannelita came over with the cat.

"Let's reenact the scene," I said, stepping back. "Pretend you've just gotten out of the car. It's dark. Show me how you locked it and went up and unlocked the front door. Take your time."

Cannelita stood by the car door.

"I got out...," she said.

"Take it slow. Put down the cat."

She put down the cat.

"What's her name?" I said.

"Tira, because she reminds me of tiramisu. The black and brown on white."

"Okay," I said. "Was your purse on your arm like it is now?"

"Yes."

"With the key in your hand? Or back in your purse?"

"In my hand."

"And you locked the car right here?"

"No, I picked up the cat."

"Okay, pick up the cat."

She picked up the cat.

"I walked around the front of the car and up the path," she said.

She did that and stopped by a rampant lavender. She turned back toward the car.

"I beeped it locked from here."

"And put the key in your purse?"

"No, because of the cat."

"Then what?"

"I went up on the porch and got the house key out from under the mat and unlocked the front door."

She carried the cat onto the porch and squatted with an oof. Her purse, hanging from her arm, settled on the concrete next to the doormat. Cradling the cat with one arm, she quickly slid a hand under the mat.

"Well, I'll be," she said.

"Car key under there?"

She stood up with the cat, the purse, the key and another oof.

I drove home with her thanks ringing in my ears. I went upstairs and did a quick check of Tommy's day, which again was spent at the track and again resulted in winnings modest in the extreme. Like other gamblers I have known, he did not give up hope.

Liesl and I drove down to Foxwoods Casino in Connecticut the second week in November. A storm up from the south brought mild temperatures and heavy rain for the weekend. My Jeep was in the shop so we rented a sporty Dodge Challenger and took I95 south to Providence. Liesl wanted to visit a German colleague on the way to the casino complex, a professor on the faculty at Brown named Otto Lehmann.

We met Lehmann for lunch downtown in a cafe at the Providence Place Mall. Before we went in, Liesl asked my permission to spend the time with him talking shop in their native tongue. When lunch was served, I ate my chicken satay and kept quiet. Our umbrellas dripped in a line, propped against the wall. By the time my plate was clean, Liesl had Otto panting with excitement. They took turns scribbling on a yellow legal pad he had fished out of a large pocket in his tweeds. They drank coffee and in the end carried their food out in doggie bags.

After Liesl sent Otto on his way, we got back on I95 and followed it south to Route 184 and Route 2 West through a stretch of old-fashioned Connecticut countryside, taking it easy in the downpour. The rain let up at North Stonington. Twenty degrees of rainbow appeared briefly between parting clouds. When the sun emerged, gray forest transformed to wet brown woods.

"Herr Lehmann seemed quite excited," I said.

"Herr Professor Lehmann, Liebchen," Liesl said.

"Sorry. What were you telling him?"

"I gave him new ideas about Umkehreinwand," she said.

"What a language," I said.

She repeated the name into her phone.

"Loschmidt's paradox," the phone said.

"Which one is that?" I said.

"The irreversibility paradox," Liesl said.

She looked at me and I wiggled my eyebrows.

"Entropy increases," she said. "The laws of thermodynamics are time-asymmetric, but the laws of physics are time-symmetric. It should not be possible to derive the fact of entropy from the laws of physics."

"Aha."

"There are many attempts to explain this. I suggested a fruitful new approach to the Herr Doctor."

She smiled at me with a warmth that made me grip the wheel a little tighter.

"When you discuss physics like you did today," I said, "are your theories figured out by yourself or based on knowledge you've acquired in the future? I asked you this before, up on the mountain."

"The theories are mine and the future's, mixed together."

"You must have learned a lot in the future. Are you sharing this with scientists like Professor Lehmann?"

"Not the scanner."

"But the rest?"

"The answer to this question is complicated."

"Complicated why? Complicated how?"

"Do you want to know the future?"

"Nothing bad."

She didn't answer.

Traffic was light. I squinted into the sun's glare on the wet road.

"Give me a hint," I said. "I don't want details. Spare me the particulars. Tell me why the answer is complicated without giving me any specifics."

"This is not possible."

"All right, forget it," I said.

We continued in silence. I was surprised at the run-down property we passed from time to time. I had assumed that the state was populated exclusively by rich and recent New York refugees.

"If you bring back knowledge from the future, isn't that a paradox?" I said. "How did it get there in the first place?"

"I explained to you how I learned about us together while I was still in Germany. Bringing knowledge from the future is all the same."

"I was wondering about that," I said. "If there are infinite universes where a Liesl finds me in some other universe and there are no time loops, how does the scanner get past those universes to reach others where you and I, and maybe Earth, don't exist?"

"In the same way that you solve Zeno's paradox by taking a single step."

A speeding pickup passed us, splattering our

windshield with water. I touched the wipers.

"So what was the fruitful idea that you offered Lehmann?" I said. "Something to do with dimensions and infinities and contiguous points in space?"

"Yes."

"How do those things solve the entropy paradox?"

"Entropy summed over all directions of time yields a null result. There is a convergence. It is why we sum over infinity."

"Infinity," I said. "Nature's all-purpose tool."

"It is so in this multiverse," Liesl said. "In higher orders, past and present may evolve. Paradoxes may be normal."

No end to it.

"We're almost there," I said.

We had bed and breakfast accommodations in Ledyard. We turned off the highway on Indiantown Road and drove until we found a white clapboard farmhouse with a discreet sign out front. I parked by a compost pile around the side and hauled our overnight bags out of the trunk. Inside, Liesl spoke with our hostess in fluent French. The woman led us out and showed us to a cottage situated next to a hibernating garden.

There were fresh flowers in our bedroom in spite of the season. We showered and dressed and drove over to Foxwoods, which was situated on the Mashantucket Pequot Reservation. We had dinner and went to a show at the Fox Theater featuring a new circus troupe. Before coming back to the bed and breakfast, we walked over to the Casino of the Wind. Liesl spent five minutes learning the rules of blackjack, house and otherwise, and another ten watching the action at one of the tables. She asked the dealer a question or two.

He answered in detail, patient with her, as were those at the table. Her aura did that.

When she sat down to play, her bets were decisive. She drew a crowd, which in time cheered frequently. A hostess served me two quick drinks. Liesl won in spite of the eight-deck shoes. Her cheeks were still flushed when I turned out the lights in our cottage. Her excitement carried over.

"You know that I love you," I said in the morning.

Liesl put her arms around me.

"It is not love," she said.

If it wasn't love, it needed a name like love.

I worked late at Lankershim the Friday after finding Cannelita's key, and got to The Studio at nine. Garza came in fifteen minutes after me. A Dodgers/Giants game had reached the seventh inning on the flat screen behind the bar. Keishi disappeared from my side when the big man entered. The other drinkers kept their eyes on the ball game or the glass in front of them. Garza dropped onto the newly vacant stool at my elbow. Mimi brought over the Red and a glass.

"Well?" Garza said, pouring himself a drink.

"Sorry," I said. "So far I've got nothing."

"You're lying," Garza said.

He wasn't speculating. He said it like he knew it.

"In my business," he said, "I hear lies all day, every day. After a while you can tell."

"I've made some progress," I said.

"I'm rating that a half-lie."

"I said before, I help you find him, you hurt him, it's on my conscience."

"We talked about that. I won't kill him. Where is he?"

"I can't tell you for sure where he is right now,

but I can call you tomorrow and tell you where he is then."

"That sounds like the truth with a little bit of lying thrown in," Garza said. "You're not telling me everything but okay, you're telling me enough. Tomorrow. Just in case, though, I know a guy. Like you, he's into computers. I'm gonna send him around. He'll help make sure you get this done."

"Don't do that."

"Hey, I'm not trying to steal your, you know, tricks of the trade or whatever. My neck is on the line here."

"I don't need help or supervision. You can trust me and if you can recognize the truth, you know that's it. And remind me again why you coughed up the twenty thousand."

Garza laughed.

"You have found him, haven't you? My mom was right. You are an amazing guy. I coughed up the twenty because Tommy never lied to me, not once. I like him. He believed everything he told me but he was wrong. Plus there's that thing where my daughter is in love with him."

"What's she saying?"

"If I hurt him, she's leaving home, but she don't mean it. If he takes off, she'll get over it."

His turn to lie and Tommy wasn't taking off, which meant Garza would have to disappear him to keep peace with both the family and the mob.

"I'll call you tomorrow," I said.

"You still got my number?"

I nodded.

"I understand you don't want me to hurt the kid," he said. "I respect that. Only sometimes life don't give us a choice."

Liesl had also told me that. Garza caught the sudden fury in my face before pain killed it.

"Please don't go," I said to Liesl over breakfast, the first Monday in December.

I swore to myself I wouldn't plead, but a week after Foxwoods I heard her on the phone to Germany and it hit me that she had one foot out the door.

We were sitting in the Forbes cafe in MIT's Stata building. Semester's end loomed. Liesl put her hand on mine, next to the syrup.

"I must return to my family and the Institute," she said.

She picked up her fork.

"You told me it wasn't love, what I feel, but it is," I said. "Got to be."

I wasn't going to say that, either.

"This is not a time for love," she said.

She busied herself with her breakfast.

"Why not?" I said.

She didn't answer.

"I want to know," I said.

"I owe you this answer," Liesl said. "I am too fond of you."

"Whoever you saw in the future, it wasn't us," I said. "We can make up our own minds. We're on a different branch. You can stay."

She put down her fork and plucked her napkin out of her lap.

"Come with me to my office, mein Schätzchen," she said.

We left the public fishbowl and hiked over to Building 6. In her office, Liesl sat down behind her desk and I perched like a freshman on the edge of a chair in front of her.

"It is not a time for love, Saul. I will explain."

I opened my mouth but she cut me off.

"I came to America for this time with you," she said. "Now I must go back to my family. Life gives no choice."

I knew it all along but I didn't want to know it.

"I must prepare for the future," Liesl said. "You also must prepare."

"Prepare how? For what?"

"There will be changes," she said.

I leaned forward.

"Everyone will have a scanner," she said.

"You're releasing it? Why would you do that?"

"I am not releasing it. Another person discovers it."

"You told Lehmann in Providence about the dimensions and their time arrows."

"The next inventor does not know my theories. He is a young man in China. The government takes his device, but skrupellose Männer sell the knowledge. The dimensions exist. Machines use them when we ask them to use them. My teaching helps prepare science for the shock caused by the scanner."

I tried to take in the notion of a world full of scanners.

"We Liesls kept it a secret," she said.

"Then what happens?"

"It is complicated. Everyone scans the future, to take advantage over others, to avoid accidents, to plan a day or a life. They make choices."

"And?"

"The worlds around us are no longer the same as ours. They... beginnen sich zu verändern."

"Begin to change," came the translator's muffled voice from Liesl's back pocket.

"Diversify," Liesl said. "They begin to diversify."
She shook her head.

"Science becomes collecting," she said, "not researching. The future is like returning to school."

"Does society survive?"

"On some worlds yes, on some worlds no."

"How should we prepare for this?"

"I do not know," Liesl said. "I am not practical."

"How soon do the scanners appear? How quickly do they spread?"

"On the early worlds, they come now in three or four years. On the late worlds, they come in ten. When they come, they spread quickly."

"Are we an early world or a late one?"

"There is no way to know."

"So this is why you came here?"

"I came here for what we have done together. I came here for all these experiences that I did not have before."

"The civilizations that survive, what do they look like?"

"It is not so simple to explain."

"Try."

"After the scanner, the transporter is discovered."

"The transporter?"

"The scanner displays. The transporter moves."

"My God. Time travel? Across the multiverse? How is that possible? Wouldn't we have seen it happening in the past? Wouldn't we see it happening now?"

"It is happening now. It has always happened. We do not see it because we experience only our three particular dimensions and their time's flow."

"You and I might be here from the future right now?"

"You do not understand. We are here now in all dimensions, moving toward infinite futures in infinite directions. We have not yet learned to perceive this, except through the scanner's mediation. Other races have learned."

"That makes no sense," I said.

"Each of us is... eine Zusammenstellung,,,"

"An assemblage," her phone said.

"...of matter and energy" Liesl said.

She thought for a moment.

"The constituents of every atom in our bodies, all the way down to the elements of our quarks, exist in an infinity of dimensions. The relationship of these constituents to each other varies. In an infinity of worlds, they compose our bodies. In an infinitely larger infinity of worlds, they are not associated. Most universes are formless and chaotic."

I held my head. Liesl sat waiting.

"What about killing my grandfather?" I finally said. "That paradox."

"You are not understanding infinity and dimension. On infinite worlds in infinite dimensions, of course you kill your grandfather. Or any other living thing. Remember Umkehreinwand. Causality follows the arrow. Jumping to another world and killing your grandfather is not a paradox. Using the transporter, the interface between known and unknown is pushed beyond human understanding, but by integrating cognition using ever more dimensions in our minds, perhaps we can understand enough to advance."

"Stop," I said. "You're going back to Germany. That's all I know."

"I am sorry."

We sat in silence. I let Liesl's coming-soon news sink in. Students passed in the hall outside, noisily.

"Then what?" I said. "Assuming we survive the scanner and transporter."

"Wir uns verstreuen... We disperse."

She fluttered a hand.

"We disperse using other dimensions," she said. "It is why we find no advanced races in this three-dimensional universe. This answers the Fermi question."

"Why do we disperse?" I said. "What's so special about where we disperse to?"

"All things are possible somewhere, mein Bärchen. Perhaps we each find our own paradise or our own heaven. Perhaps we find ways to higher-level multiverses. Perhaps the infinite is an aspect of the eternal."

"I'm coming to Germany."

"Now you surprise me."

I stood up. Liesl pointed at the chair. I sat down.

"I seek truth," Liesl said, "but the infinite defies truth. Every theory is true somewhere. Every idea is true. Now I return to my family and the Institute to find a new philosophy. I have lived this life with you. I must go back."

"I could use a new philosophy myself," I said.

"I think your philosophy is okay now for you."

Maybe I had the right philosophy but I didn't have the girl.

After Garza left the bar Friday night with my promise to call him on Saturday, I sat for a while, thinking. Mimi let me be. Presently, I got up and left.

Outside, a jumbo jet rumbled overhead, lifting off from Bob Hope airport. Jekell and Bush were nowhere to be seen. Warm air pulsed against me, the wake of a passing truck. I got in the Jeep and drove home, blind sober.

In my apartment, I found an unopened bottle of bourbon, filled a bucket with ice cubes, and washed out a tumbler. I dropped cubes into the tumbler and carried it and the bottle into the scanner room. Sat down in my easy chair and put the glass and bottle on the lamp table beside me. Thought about the future. Thought about Liesl, working at the Institute and waiting for the deluge with her mama and papa. Thought about Garza and Tommy and Julieta. I hefted the unopened bottle. A long, empty night lay ahead. I opened the bottle.

Across the room, the scanner sat silent, a box with an answer for every question and infinite questions for every answer, waiting for me like a crazy fortune teller. I splashed bourbon into the glass. Its bouquet filled the room. I took my first sip before the liquid cooled over the cubes.

The past is friendly. No tricks. Finding Malika's cat, the dog pooping on Agnes' lawn, a neighborhood graffiti tagger. The future fans out unseen in a snarl of worlds where nuggets of good news drown in a sea of entropy. We're born in the past. We die in the future.

I drained the glass and filled it again.

The beauty of drinking, if you drink enough, is that it's not about what's happening or what's going to happen. It's about what has happened, what's not happening, and what's never going to happen. Everything may be true somewhere, but that somewhere wasn't in my bottle.

Was the transporter good news? I could find a Liesl in the multiverse who stuck around, but I'd find me there too.

I had it all wrong. Humanity's path didn't stretch into the distant future, at least not in this batch of universes. The transporter changed everything. If the country survived, I'd be travelling through time and space in every direction searching for love and eternity.

I heaved out of the chair and carried my glass and the bottle across to the scanner table. I wouldn't be needing the ice.

I didn't want heavenly realms. I wanted Liesl in this one.

I switched on the console, pulled on my headset, positioned the keyboard in front of me, and nestled the master controller in my lap.

I scanned Tommy's Friday. It unspooled much like his Thursday. He nursed his roll at the track, made a few bucks, didn't hit on any of his plunges. When night fell, he drove over to Shadow Hills for a thirty-minute assignation with Julietta, two blocks from her home. She slipped out to meet him on foot.

I watched them for a minute and then hopped to Santa Anita using the coordinates I had bookmarked the night before. The track was lit up. The groundskeepers were grooming the dirt and grass courses. I positioned myself in the infield facing the tote board, my back to the grandstand.

I jacked up the scan rate, moving into the future for the first time ever. Saturday morning arrived. The sky brightened in the east, the sun rose red, and the tote board lit up. I paused the scan at one in afternoon, post time for the first race. No meteor had destroyed the earth. No earthquake had struck.

I bookmarked my time, location, and the world thread.

I fumbled a little with the headset on, finding my glass. Took a swallow. Took a moment to wonder what effect worldwide scanners would have on horse racing and sports in general. Threads would diverge but the horses wouldn't run any faster. Hard to see how the sport of kings could survive.

I toasted the horses. Racetracks were dying anyway. I thought about jumping ahead ten or twenty years to see if Santa Anita was still in business, but I was depressed enough already. Life was my horse race.

I put down my glass before I became too philosophical to move.

For now, using the world's only scanner, I settled for recording Saturday's finishes. If no long shots came in, I would have a problem.

I watched the first race, waited for "Unofficial" to change to "Official" on the tote board, which it did. Being new to the future, I hopped across nearby threads to check the board on random worlds. No change in the results. I captured the board image.

I repeated the process for the following eight races. When I was done, I transferred the images to my phone. They included a couple of large payouts. I thought about confirming that Tommy was at the track but I didn't want to see myself there. I wasn't ready for that, even half-drunk.

I powered down the scanner and pulled off my headset. My first visit to the future, concluded. No spoilers.

I didn't plan on a second visit.

I arrived at the Branford Senior Center in Panorama City at eight o'clock Saturday morning. I worked half days on Saturday but on this one I headed out early at eleven. My Jeep was parked in the lot behind the center. I had two hundred dollars in my pocket, enough for parking and general admission at the track, a couple of bets, a light lunch, and drinks. I could also share a couple bucks with Tommy if he ran out of money too soon.

I climbed into the Jeep, pulled on my Angel's cap, and sat waiting to get out of the lot while Mr. and Mrs. Sramek crept into it in their thirty-year-old neat-as-a-pin Camaro.

The Hollywood Freeway was congested and I made my way south to the Ventura and east to Pasadena at a slow but steady speed. The day was warm and clear.

Sitting in the Branford office, I had reviewed my tote-board pics. I hoped that since my heart was pure and I was using my future data to save Tommy's life, the gods of irony would leave me alone.

Santa Anita race track is located east of Pasadena at the foot of the San Gabriel mountains, off the Foothill Freeway in Arcadia. The neighborhood hadn't changed much since my high-school days. I had planned to take Liesl to Suffolk Downs in East Boston to watch the ponies run, but the meeting was cancelled due to poor attendance the previous year.

Liesl left on the third Monday in December. A foot of fresh snow covered Cambridge. The school offered her a limo but I drove her over to Logan in the Jeep. Neither of us said much on the way, probably for different reasons. A cohort of the school's top thinkers and administrators tried to join us at the gate but Liesl and the TSA forbade it. She had the juice to get me past security, but I sat next to her at the gate in a funk. After trying once or twice to make small talk, she left me to myself.

She didn't take the scanner. Didn't need it, she said, didn't want it. I spent the rest of the week drinking and working my way through a bottle of OxyContin eighties I had picked up in Harvard Square. Seemed to make sense. I was in pain.

Still alive after that, I loaded the scanner's server and peripherals into the back of the Jeep. I stuffed some clothes in a bag and drove across the continent to LA. I spent a week with my sister in Torrance before moving into the apartment in North Hollywood. My parents and brother reached out, but I wasn't in the mood to explain anything to anyone.

I arrived at Santa Anita in plenty of time for the first race. I parked in the Gate 8 lot as Tommy had done. There were plenty of cars in the lot for the weekend's racing. More than I expected with tracks failing around the nation. I didn't spot Tommy's Cutlass. I regretted not checking the night before to confirm he had showed up.

Santa Anita's art-deco buildings, Persian green and chiffon yellow, stood unchanged with skinny palm trees stationed around them, crowns high against a sky the color of periwinkles. I bought a general admission. I wouldn't need clubhouse or infield access while dealing with the impoverished Tommy. Inside I rented a pair of binoculars.

I headed directly for Paddock Gardens. The crowd on the grass and walkways strolled about in the sun. I had no trouble spotting Tommy by the Seabiscuit statue, waiting to check out the horses in the first race. He looked Hollywood Amish in his sunglasses, fake beard and big straw hat. It was twelve-thirty, half an hour to post time.

I walked over and stood next to him. He was as tall as Garza but half as thick. I edged into the fringes of his personal space. He looked up from his Racing Form, back down, back up. I met his glance, or my glance reflecting off his shades.

"Can I help you?" he said.

He was just a kid.

"Why not wear a sign that says I'm In Disguise?" I said.

He didn't tense up. A true gambler, he remained impassive.

"You're Tommy Link," I said. "What the hell are you doing out here?"

He checked to see if I was alone, craning his neck to look around.

"Actually, the question's rhetorical," I said.

"You working for Tony?" he said.

"In a way."

"He know I'm here?"

"If he knew you were here, you wouldn't be here."

"Tony promised he wouldn't hurt me too bad."

"That was before his daughter told him if he hurt you, she'd move out. With your debt hanging over his head and his daughter's attitude, he's only got one play at this point."

Tommy's shoulders slumped.

"I told Julieta not to tell him that," he said. "I begged her to let me take a beating. I've got it coming. She wouldn't listen. She's afraid he'll cripple me by accident or turn me into a vegetable. She don't understand Tony can't let me walk."

"She told him what she told him and you're still here?"

"He'd look for me in Reno or Vegas or wherever I went."

"Go somewhere without casinos. You're trying to quit, why go to Vegas?"

"Everybody's got casinos. How do you know

I'm trying to quit?"

"I have friends in GA."

"Hey, that's supposed to be confidential."

"Let's stay focused here."

"I'm quitting as soon as I climb out of the hole. I'm here because I'm in love. I can't start running now, for crissakes. I've got to pay Tony what I owe him."

"You think you're going to climb out of your hole here?"

"Where else can I?"

"Why not buy a lottery ticket? Same odds."

He stood a little taller.

"Very funny," he said. "I've got no choice, man. If you're not going to call Garza, leave me alone. I need to think."

The horses for the first race were led out to circle the walking ring.

"Who do you like in this one?" I said.

"Leave me alone."

He studied the horses as they passed.

"Garza told me that poker and team sports are your specialties," I said.

"Poker and team sports got me into this fake beard. Leave me alone."

"I like the two horse in this one," I said.

"The two horse is the favorite," Tommy said. "I can't make what I need betting favorites. I've got to hit a trifecta or Pick Six on a long shot."

"Not going to happen in this race," I said.

"You can't tell with the cheap horses."

"That's the problem," I said.

"Leave me alone."

The first race was a claimer full of unreliable three- and four-year-olds, horses that hadn't won more than one race. They were all available for sale after the race at the claiming price, in this case five thousand dollars. No one can handicap the early races at a track, though many have tried. Not the professionals, though. They sell advice but don't take it.

After the horses had passed, Tommy picked one based on its trainer, who, according to Tommy, was known for buying losers and turning them into winners. We walked out to the apron in front of the grandstand, found some shade, and waited for the horses to warm up on the track.

I let Tommy think, or worry, in peace. The horses came through from the paddock and trotted back and forth in front of us. To my untrained eye, Tommy's horse seemed a little washy. I held my tongue. Tommy went in to bet. The horses circled to the back of the track. Tommy came out. The horses were loaded into the gate. I put the glasses on them.

The start was clean and after some doubt in the scrum that followed the first turn, the favorite won going away.

The number two went up on the infield board. "Unofficial" changed to "Official." Tommy tore up his tickets.

"Uh oh," I said. "That didn't last long."

"You called it," Tommy said.

"But didn't touch it," I said.

"Garza isn't looking for you," he said.

We headed back to the paddock and evaluated the horses for the second race. The Saturday crowd was still building, folks looking to score like Tommy rather than pros scouting around for late mail.

"I like the seven," I said. "A not-so-long shot."

"I'll bet the Exacta for the seven and the one," he said.

"Nah," I said. "Box the seven with the two favorites. You'll win a few shekels to keep you going. Forget the one."

Back on the apron, I bought us both a beer and we watched the warm-up for the second race. Kids ran around shouting at each other.

"It's like Disneyland," I said, "and we're not even on the infield."

The one horse trotted past.

"Sore," I said. "Choppy stride."

Tommy went in to bet and came back with his tickets in his pocket.

Another clean start. The seven horse was a swooper, running in the back of the pack until he burst away on the outside to win. The two favorites followed. I put the glasses on the horses after the finish and watched them walk off, sweat on their hides, foam on their lips.

The one horse finished out of the money. The crowd on the apron receded.

Tommy tore up his tickets.

"You bet the one horse?" I said.

"I told you, I need the odds. You've got an eye for horses, though. That's two in a row."

"It's not my eye," I said. "I've got the feeling."

Tommy nodded.

"Why didn't you bet?" he said.

"I don't bet the cheap races. You ever get the feeling?"

"Why I gamble."

"You get it out here yet?"

"What do you think?"

We dropped our bottles in a recycle receptacle and walked back to the paddock.

In the third, I touted two of the finishers but

threw in a ringer. Tommy boxed the three horses for a Trifecta ticket. The bet covered the six possibilities in which the three horses all finished. He shouted as two of the three charged down the stretch well ahead of the rest. I kept my glasses on the ringer, who was well placed and stalking the pace. Moving outside a rival, the horse took an awkward step onto the dirt crossing, drifted four wide into the stretch, and was pulled up by his jockey passing the midstretch. He walked off limping.

Tommy tore up his tickets but his blood was up.

"We had that into the stretch!" he said. "What's your name, anyway?"

"Saul."

"Well, Saul, this could be our day! Closest I've come so far."

On the way back to the paddock, I shook my head.

"Not feeling it for the fourth," I said. "Let's sit this one out."

Tommy groaned but bowed to my gut. I walked us over to the Bud Light Lounge in the paddock.

"You have an ID?" I said.

"Sure."

He produced it, a California license that rendered him twenty-one. He could bet at the track at eighteen, but he needed the license to bet in the sports books, casinos and clubs, along with a little forbearance from the proprietors.

I paid the lounge walk-in fee and we took seats by a window looking down on the paddock and the walking ring. We ordered beer and visited the buffet. I spooned a little potato salad onto my plate and forked a chicken leg over to keep it company. Tommy, a growing lad on the run, loaded his plate.

We ate and drank fast, listening to the click of billiard balls mixed with crowd chatter. The fourth race went off on the monitors. We skipped the fifth as well, Tommy restive but staying true to the gods of luck and the memory of my start. The order of finish in both races matched my phone list. Modest payoffs in both.

We returned to the paddock for the sixth, an allowance race featuring horses of a higher class, but not yet ready for stakes racing.

"Give me your paper," I said to Tommy.

He handed it to me and I turned to the sixth race and studied the page. Tommy fidgeted beside me.

"What do you think?" he said.

"Two, three, five, six, ten," I said. "Buy the one-twenty ticket. The ten horse will go off at forty to one and the five horse at thirty to one. Our race."

The sixth was the designated Super Hi-5, with a one-dollar bet in which the five top finishers are to be picked in order. No one had picked a winning combination Thursday or Friday and the carryover money to the Saturday pool was excellent. A hundred-and-twenty dollar ticket allowed the bettor to box five horses, that is, cover all possible finishes that included the five of them.

Tommy was sweating like a race horse, appropriately, and hanging on my every word.

"Two, three, five, six, ten," he said.

My earlier choices had him amped. The size of his bet compared to the size of his diminished poke had him amped. The moment of truth had arrived and I too was amped. Every branch world I had checked Friday night showed this race finishing ten, five, six, two, three. There would be a few worlds where that didn't happen for one reason or another, but not many. The odds against us were infinitesimal, given the width of the band containing the worlds I had examined. However, bad beats live in the dark heart of gambling. Highly improbable negative outcomes somehow seem more natural than big wins.

I accompanied Tommy to the tellers. We stood in different lines. I bet two bucks on a loser. When we came back outside, Tommy had the gambler's calm that comes after the life-or-death bet has been laid.

I handed him the binoculars.

The start of the race was good. The ten horse went off at forty to one. The five came up on his heels at the three-quarters pole, eager to run. The ten took a short lead into the stretch and inched away in midstretch, kicking clear under a steady hand ride with Tommy screaming beside me. The five horse finished two lengths back with the six on his flank. The two and three faded enough to give us a scare but hung on to produce a winning ticket for Tommy.

We waited for the signal that the race was official and to see the Super Hi-5 payout. The stewards certified the race. A one-dollar bet that correctly picked the five finishers in order paid $9,445 from a pool of $98,151.

Tommy stood there weeping.

"How much did you put on your box?" I said.

"Four tickets."

"So you're forty thousand richer."

He looked around himself as if he were waking up.

"So far," he said.

"It's about knowing when to quit," I said.

"Not on a day like today it isn't. You won too. No way we stop."

I took out my phone and called Garza.

"I found him," I said.

"Where?"

"Santa Anita."

"Sure," Garza said. "I'm on my way. Where are you parked? Bring him out."

"Come in and get him," I said. "We'll be in the Bud Light."

"Garza?" Tommy said when I returned the phone to my pocket.

I nodded.

"He'll settle for it," Tommy said.

"Good thing he has a daughter."

"Yeah."

We went back inside and sat down at the same table and drank beer while we waited. Outside, the horses circled the paddock for the seventh race.

"How about this one?" Tommy said, eyeing the monitor and the voucher machines along the wall.

"We're done," I said. "Call your sponsor. In the meantime, I'm your substitute sponsor."

"Or my dad."

"I'm the guy who just saved your life, which is more than you can say for your dad."

"And I appreciate it, but we can still get rich. Three more races."

"You're rehabbing, remember?"

"Forget that," Tommy said. "I'll rehab tomorrow. Let me get well first. The Tony thing was only half of it. Julieta and I need a nest egg. Don't quit on me now."

"Tommy," I said. "Call your sponsor. Then call Julieta. No more bets."

The horses headed out to the track. Tommy leaned forward, elbows on the table. His eyes jumped from mine to the monitor behind me.

"Call your sponsor," I said.

"I don't need him, or you," he said.

"Yeah?"

He pulled out his Racing Form.

"Who do you like in the seventh?" I said. "You've got a couple of minutes."

He stared at the paper and shook his head.

"What if I call Julieta and my sponsor?" he said. "What if I explain what we've got going here? What if they both give me the go-ahead?"

"This is Julieta and your sponsor you're talking about?" I said.

He went back to the Racing Form, which shook in his hands. He glanced up at me from time to time.

"Just give me a hint," he said.

When I didn't reply, he got up and stalked over to the window. On the monitor, the horses headed for the starting gate. Tommy got someone on the phone. He began talking. He talked faster as the horses were loaded into their barriers.

The seventh race was one and a sixteenth miles in distance. I looked up at the monitor when I heard the bell. I had the finish on my phone as eight, five, four, two. I figured the payout on a four-horse exacta bet at over a million. Tommy didn't need that, nor did Garza, nor did I.

The race was well contended. On the turn, the eight horse's jockey stepped out for room on the outside. The five horse, another long shot, was off his right hip and the eight gave him a little bump, then closed steadily on the two and the four to take control in the final sixteenth and finish going away. The race ended eight, five, four, two, as my phone predicted. Tommy was lucky. Ignorance is bliss.

I took in some beer. Tommy talked on, phone to ear, pacing and gesticulating, rapping his knuckles on the window glass. Presently, a murmur passed through the room. I looked up at the monitor. The finish was not official. The jockey on the five horse had not objected to the bump on the turn but the stewards had posted an inquiry. On the replay, the incident looked to be minor between the two horses. I thought the jockey on the five might have stopped riding for a couple of strides but I didn't think that this in any way affected the outcome of the race. On a major track like Santa Anita, the stewards tended to let the horses run.

Tommy returned his phone to his pocket. As he started back to our table, the eight was taken down. The horse was disqualified for bothering the five. The disqualification was an aberration, caused by a steward with animus toward the horse or its owner or trainer or jockey, or who was just having a bad day. A phantom call.

"They said okay," Tommy said, standing on the other side of the table. "Julieta and my sponsor, they said OKAY."

"Uh huh."

Garza came through the door looking like a man about to shoot his dog. Below us, the horses for the eighth race were led out. Garza walked over to our table and sat down. Tommy sat down. I couldn't read murder in Garza's face but it was no time for a sunny hello.

Tommy reached into his pocket and brought out his winning ticket. He handed it to Garza.

"Forty thousand, give or take," he said, "before taxes."

Garza stared at the ticket. He looked up with a mixed expression of skepticism and profound relief.

"Let's go cash it in," he said to Tommy. "I'll let you do it. You're in a lower bracket."

We stood up.

"My mom was right about you," Garza said to me.

He handed me a wad of cash.

"Happy ending," he said.

"Goodbye, Tommy," I said to the boy.

He gave me a pleading look. His life had been preserved but he was missing out on half a dream payday. Gamblers Anonymous had its work cut out for it.

Garza took Tommy's arm and led him off to the short line. I let a couple of minutes pass before heading out. In the parking lot, I stopped for a moment and looked up at the sky. Cloudless. Nothing had changed. Same old world.

Only it wasn't. I was standing on a planet where the eight horse lost. That had to make some kind of difference.

I drove back to North Hollywood and stopped in at The Studio. Keishi and Juan Lopez were nursing late-afternoon beers at the bar. Walt was on his stool. He nodded to me when I came in. I eased down next to Keishi.

"Why is this place called The Studio?" I asked him.

"It got the name in the Thirties but why I don't know," he said.

"We're in North Hollywood," Juan said.

"Which is nowhere near Hollywood," Keishi said.

"Disney is down at the end of Buena Vista," Juan said. "Warner Brothers and Universal are down Olive."

"On the other side of the freeway," Keishi said.

"No freeway there in the Thirties," Juan said.

Mimi joined Walt behind the bar. Walt stood up and removed his apron.

"You got some sun today," Mimi said to me.

"I was out at Santa Anita."

"I haven't been there in ages. How'd you make out?"

"Couple lucky picks."

"I'd like to go out there sometime."

"How about tomorrow?" I said.

"Let's not rush it," she said.

J. H. Malone has had three careers: High energy particle research in Boston and Los Alamos, social work in San Francisco, and tech writing for startups in Silicon Valley. Over the past years Malone has placed science fiction, crime, romance, and other stories, as well as movie reviews, in two dozen Internet and print publications.

Thank you to the Wapshott Press sponsors, supporters, and Friends of the Wapshott Press.

Muna Deriane
Kit Ramage
Rachel Livingston
Ann and John Brantingham
Marilyn Robertson
Toni Rodriguez
James and Rebecca White
Leslie Bohem
David Meischen
James Wilson
Kathleen Warner
Robert Earle and Mary Azoy
Kathleen Bonagofsky
Suzanne Siegel
Phil Temples
Richard Whittaker
Ann Siemens
Elaine Padilla
Laurel Sutton
John Grigor Bell

The Wapshott Press is a 501(c)(3) not-for-profit enterprise publishing work by emerging and established authors and artists. We publish books that should be published. We are very grateful to the people who believe in our plans and goals, as well as our hopes and dreams. Our new website is at www. WapshottPress.org. Donations gratefully accepted at www.Donate.WapshottPress.org.

www.ingramcontent.com/pod-product-compliance
Lightning Source LLC
Chambersburg PA
CBHW070533130626
46555CB00003B/1391